MARK PRI

THE FOOLISH KING

Illustrated by

MARTIN BROWN

Inked and coloured by Geraint Ford

To my beautiful daughter, Holly, for whom I invented this story one sunny day at Orchard Coombe

— Mark Price

To Ruth

— Martin Brown

Contents

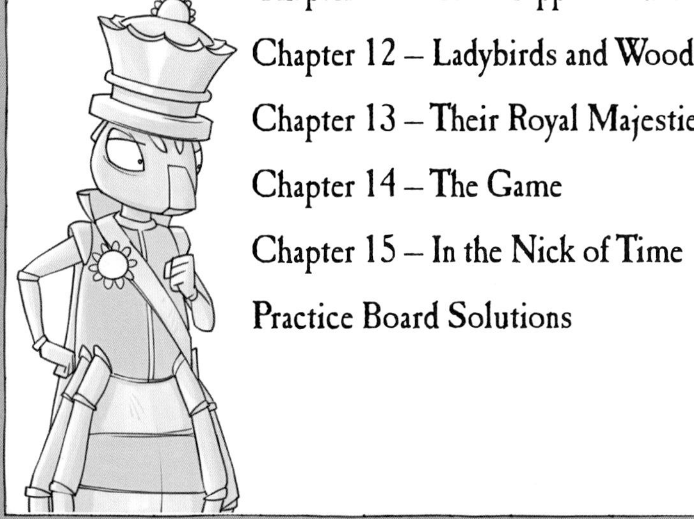

A Key to the Chess Pieces

Chess pieces look a little different nowadays – here's a guide to how they looked when the magical game of chess was first discovered . . .

Ants and Bees

The Queen

The King

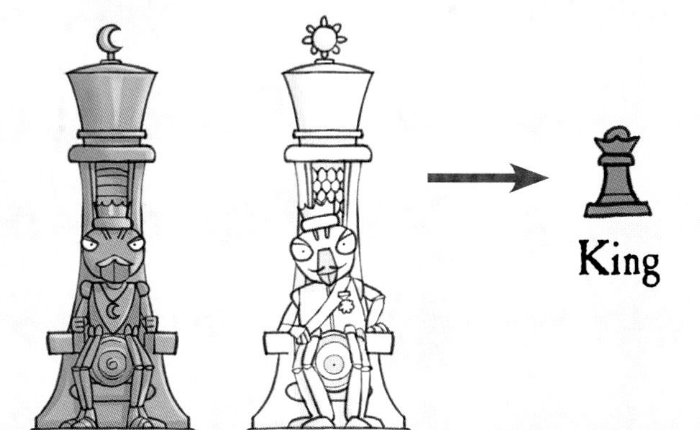

You can also learn and play chess with the Foolish King app!
Or you can play at www.thefoolishking.com

Grasshoppers and Crickets!

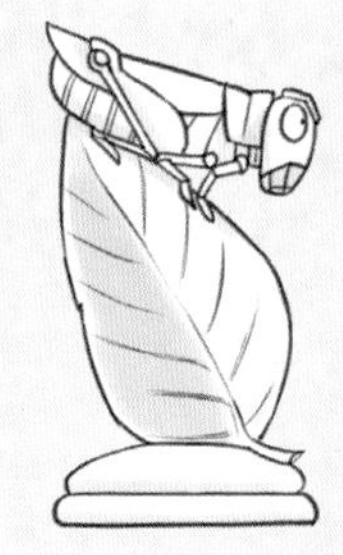

Knight

Worms and Slugs!

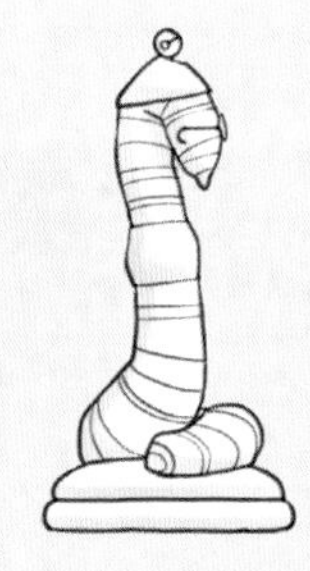

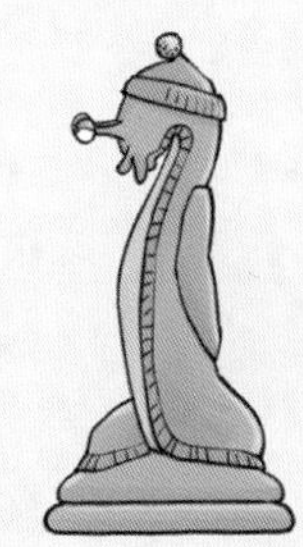

Bishop

Ladybirds and Woodlice

Castle

How The World's Greatest Game Began

Some say the game of chess was invented in ancient China, some say a very clever Maharaja from India thought it up, yet the board pieces in front of you come from even earlier than that. They have been reshaped and changed many times through history. Kings and queens, bishops and knights have all played this ancient game, but none of them knew its secret history.

This is the story of chess, a story lost in the mists of time, which tells of a far away kingdom and two children, Holly and Pip, and the part they played in discovering the game. We'll meet those two soon, but every story must start at the beginning . . .

Chapter 1
THE GOLDEN PEAR

Shortly before time began, when dragons still filled the sky and birds and even insects could talk, good King Marra ruled the Kingdom of Stur. King Marra was a great ruler: just, kind and wise. The gentle king loved his people and they loved him in return. His chief adviser was an ancient snowy owl called Woogle, who, like all owls, was very clever and wise.

King Marra loved to garden. He patiently showed his people how to care for their gardens and fields and so the kingdom prospered and flourished. King Marra particularly liked pears, and each year he held a competition to see who could grow the biggest and juiciest fruit. He would reward the winning gardener with The Golden Pear for their trouble. Everyone tried so hard to win.

Two children, called Holly and Pip, tried especially hard. They lived in the royal garden next to King Marra's palace. Mr Perry, their dad, was the king's head gardener and they did everything they could to help him win.

The royal garden was the most magnificent of all the gardens, with the biggest of all pear trees at the bottom. It was King Marra's pride and joy. Mr Perry was a huge man, with big rough hands the size of shovels and green fingers from a lifetime of gardening. He had won The Golden Pear more times than anyone could remember. One more win would make him the all-time champion!

Holly and Pip loved growing up in such a wonderful garden and exploring every nook and cranny. They became as knowledgeable as their father about the plants and the insects that helped the plants to grow. Holly was very clever, sensible and always reading. Pip liked to explore, especially the branches of the huge pear tree, and was always discovering new things. And like all children, they both loved playing games!

Every day Mr Perry worked hard in the garden, planting, raking and watering. And the creatures helped. The bees and butterflies fluttered from plant to plant, feeding on sweet nectar and spreading pollen. The slugs and snails nibbled on the dying plants, leaving space for new ones. Everything worked in harmony and everything grew well. Everyone was happy.
But there was one thing that really worried the king. It was his son, Royal Prince Parip.

Chapter 2

THE ROTTEN APPLE

Growing up in a royal palace, Prince Parip had become used to everyone waiting on him hand and foot. Nobody dared disagree with him, as he had the most terrible temper. Worse still, he was greedy, mean and jealous. Although his father tried to teach him to be kind and interested in others he only cared about himself, and even more terrible was that he thought gardening beneath him. Despite his father's gentle lessons, Plump Parip, as people called him, would laugh as slugs exploded into slimy bits under his feet, giggle when he pulled the legs off spiders, and roar with laughter as he shook the half-grown fruit off the trees. Then his favourite game was to stamp on it all and smash it to bits.

Parip's constant companion was Crow.
Parip had found Crow as a fledgling in
a flowerbed, scoffing hard-working earthworms,
and instantly liked him!

As a child, Parip loved playing games, but no one would play with him. Other children didn't like the awful tantrums when he lost. It was easier to let him win, or not to play with him at all! So Parip spent most of his time with Crow thinking up mean games and tricks, like putting glue on flower heads so that when the bees landed for pollen they got stuck. Or pouring water down ant holes, when they were mixing the soil, and counting how many dead ants would float to the top. And firing poor snails over the castle wall with his catapult while Crow tried to catch them in his beak. Woogle, the king's owl, worried more and more about what would happen when Parip became king and Crow was his adviser.

King Marra ruled until a wrinkly old age. Every day he hoped that Prince Parip would learn to love the gardens and insects as much as he did. Maybe some of what he had taught might stick. But as the king looked out of his castle window one last time before he died, he saw his son shaking all the unripe pears out of the king's prize pear tree. A tear ran down his face as he beckoned over his faithful servant, Woogle. "Promise to help Prince Parip be a good ruler. Help him to change and to love our kingdom. I have failed, my friend, but Parip is still my son and the apple of my eye. Now everything rests with you, my good and faithful wise owl," said the king with his final breath.

Woogle crossed her wings and promised to do her best, but she had a worried look in her wise old bird eyes that seemed to say that she didn't think Parip was a very rosy apple! *More like a crab apple!* thought Woogle.

Woogle was right. The new King Parip was very ambitious. He wanted to be grander and greater and more admired than his father. Instead of visiting the gardens of Stur and advising his people, he made them hold great banquets in his honour. If he didn't think the food was magnificent enough he would order the cooks to be thrown into the dungeons. Who knew what would happen to them there?

And unlike his father, King Parip had no interest in pears, or fruit-growing competitions. "Pears are silly and stupid and a waste of my time. I have far better things to do than tell smelly farmers how nice their fruit is. And I'm not wasting money on giving away Golden Pears. I shall spend that money on beautiful clothes and carriages and throw wonderful parties just for me. Then all the people will love me more because I look so nice and have such fun."

"Quite right, Your Great Cleverness," said Crow, but then he was a very bad apple, rotten to the core in fact. Woogle tried to persuade Parip that Stur needed to grow food but the king wouldn't listen.

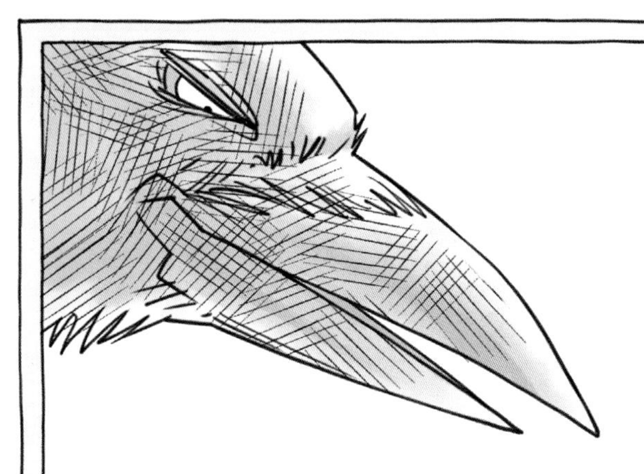

Chapter 3
THE INSECTS DEPART

All the people started to fear King Parip. Some even began to move away from Stur because he took so little interest in the land. Less and less grew in Stur so there was less and less food for everyone to eat. Greedy King Parip commanded that more and more of the food grown be used for his enormous banquets. Of course nobody wanted to go to royal parties because the king was so bad-tempered and so most of the food was thrown away. King Parip could see that he was losing the goodwill of his people. He just couldn't see why! He began to lose his temper at the slightest thing. One day, when he saw a worm eating a fallen apple at the end of his garden, he rushed forward and angrily jumped on it, exploding both the apple and the worm into hundreds of slimy wet bits. Yuck!

Creepy Crow quickly leaped forward and gobbled up the bits of worm. Even more yucky!

"How dare that little worm eat my food!" said the jealous king to Crow. "I decree that any insect eating my food will be punished."

Whoever heard of punishing insects? What a crazy idea!

"I will make sure that happens to all the insects, Your Magnificence," said the creepy Crow, even though he had no idea how to punish insects. He did like eating them though. Perhaps he thought he could eat them all. Soon he became the fattest crow in history because he gave gobbling them all up a good go!

The insects didn't like that one bit and decided to go elsewhere. Nobody knew where they were going. It was a mystery. Little by little all the insects disappeared from the fields and gardens until there were hardly any left to pollinate the plants or enrich the soil.

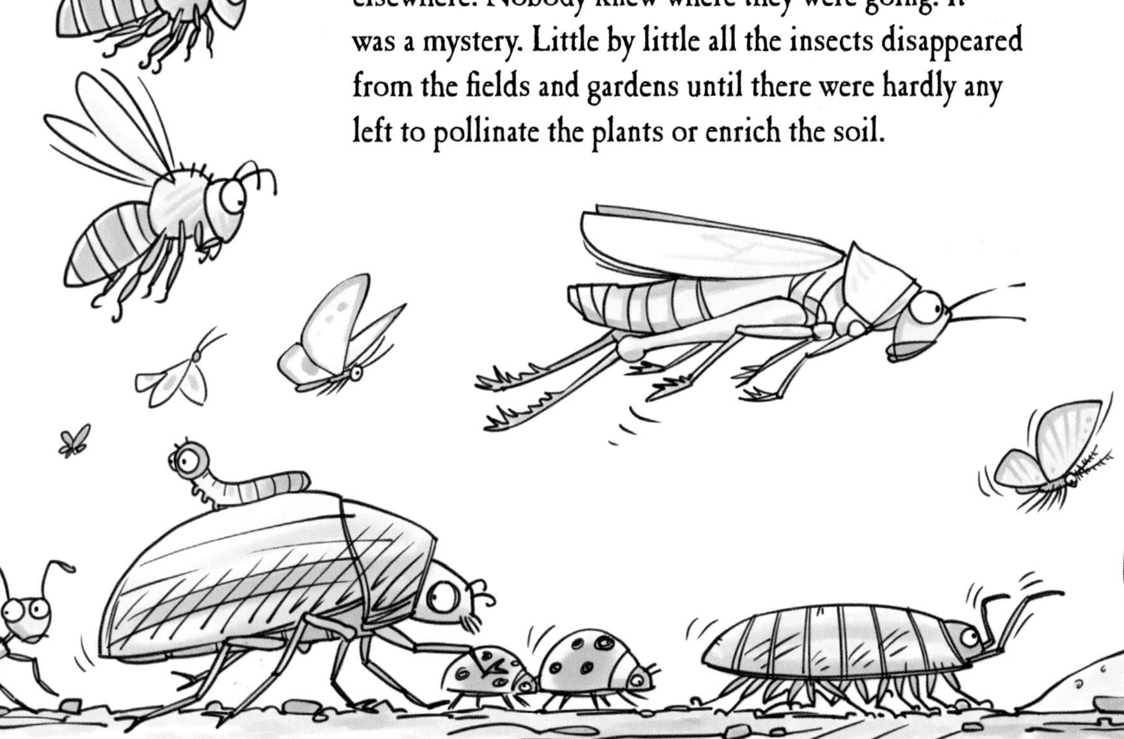

"We don't need those unimportant silly little insects," said Parip to Crow when he heard the news. "They are ugly and messy and yucky. I am sure the Court Magician can make some potions to help things grow."

"You are so right, Your Utter Brilliance, I will instruct him to do so right now," said Crow.

But the potions couldn't replace the hard-working insects. Rather than help things grow they upset the remaining insects and turned the rivers bright red. Before long the countryside was full of dead plants and the crops stopped growing completely.

There was, however, one place where plants still grew. That was the royal gardens. There, Mr Perry worked day and night just to keep a little food on the royal table. He kept the compost heap for the worms and the beetle bank that he had built up with King Marra, and with his wonderful kindness to all creatures he managed to persuade a few insects to stay. But even with his great gardening skills he couldn't grow much.

With fewer crops being grown and sold, the king started to run out of money, and his castle started to crumble. Boards covered broken windows, carriages with damaged wheels stood abandoned and awaiting repair, and there was hardly anyone to be seen. Many of the hungry people of Stur had gone away – who knows where? The king had become very thin and his once-splendid coat was now fastened with string. His breeches, now scruffy and patched, were held up by cord. With no gold to pay them, all the king's servants left, leaving only a very thin Woogle and a very fat Crow.

King Parip was becoming crosser and crosser. "I want gold and I want gold now!" demanded King Parip and he commanded Crow to collect taxes from the people. Woogle tried to explain that the farmers had little money and barely enough food for themselves. But Crow carried on anyway and took their farms instead if they had no money. That just made things worse, as more farmers and their families left Stur, and their once bountiful farms were left abandoned. Stur became poor and the people unhappy and afraid of their king.

The kingdom was in a terrible mess, and King Parip continued to blame everyone but himself for the land's misfortune.

Chapter 4
THE FINAL STRAW

One morning, King Parip awoke early, the sun pouring through the moth-eaten holes in his curtains. He felt especially hungry, tired and angry. He shouted for Woogle and Crow, who quickly flew to join him.

"Where's my breakfast?" demanded King Parip.

"I am very sorry, Your Majesty," said Woogle, bowing as low as she could. "This morning, there is no breakfast. There is nothing left in the royal kitchens. There is no breakfast at all."

"NO BREAKFAST!" roared the king. "Whoever heard of a kingdom without breakfast."

Crow didn't say anything. He bowed low too, but underneath his wing, he smirked; he knew Woogle was in trouble.

"I want to know why nothing in my kingdom grows," said the king. "And if you can't tell me, I am going to have you both plucked and roasted and served for my breakfast."

Crow saw his chance to worm himself even further into the king's favour and save his own feathers.

"Your Marvellous Magnificence," he began. "I have the answer. It's not your fault at all, sire. Look at your royal garden. Everything still grows there. How can that be while the rest of your kingdom is so poor? Mr Perry must be cheating you. His wife still makes *him* breakfast. She cooks *him* big pies while you go hungry. And have you seen those two greedy children of his? They just eat a big breakfast AND then do no work and play games all day."

"You are right," said the king. "I used to love playing games," he added wistfully.

Woogle shook her head in disbelief, as she knew how hard Mr Perry worked.

"That's not fair," she said.

"I'll tell you what's not fair," replied the king, and he shouted in Woogle's face, "It's not fair that I don't have big parties any more, or new clothes and there's NO breakfast!"

"I bet the Perrys are having a lovely big breakfast right now," screeched Crow.

As usual Mr Perry had woken before it was light to start work. He was exhausted and worried as he collapsed into his chair at the kitchen table for some well-earned breakfast.
Just then there was a loud banging on the kitchen door.
"Open up in the name of the king!"

Holly dashed to answer it and saw a very cross-looking King Parip with Crow on his shoulder. They barged into the tiny kitchen.

"Can I smell freshly baked pie?" asked the king as the smell from the oven wafted towards the open door.

"I told you, sire," said Crow. "There is no one going hungry here. See how well they all look!"

With that, King Parip exploded. His face red with rage, he screamed, "How dare you live in my cottage, in my palace grounds and not grow lots of vegetables for me! That is your job!"

"I'm working as hard as I can, but nothing is growing properly, you need the insects, we have to look after the plants together . . ." Mr Perry tried to explain.

"And the pie?" croaked Crow. "Was that made out of thin air?"

"It's a pear pie from a few pears grown by that old tree at the bottom of the garden," Mrs Perry explained. "Please share it with us!"

"And are there any other pears?" asked the king crossly.

"Just a few, right at the top, we couldn't get to them," said Pip eagerly. The king frowned at him.

"We'll get them by cutting it down, then," he said. Mr Perry shook his head sadly and started to say something, but a sudden twist of Crow's beak made him decide to hold his tongue.

"We'll have this pie, for now," said the king, snatching up the plate. "And I'll be back tomorrow."

Chapter 5

A PLAN IS HATCHED

"Did he say he's going to chop down our favourite tree?" asked a very worried-looking Pip.

"We'll think of something," said Mrs Perry, trying to sound comforting. "Now, your father and I have some important things to talk about, so why don't you both go outside and play."

In the garden, the children saw a sad-looking Woogle perched on a fence.

"What's wrong?" asked Holly. Woogle shrugged her shoulders and told Holly and Pip all about the promise she had made to King Parip's father and what had happened that morning. "I have let down King Marra," said Woogle sadly. "It's all hopeless."

"Let's go for a walk," said Holly. "Maybe we'll come up with something."

Woogle shook her head sadly, but she perched herself on Holly's shoulder and they started off. They walked until the end of the garden and sat under the doomed pear tree.

"He can't cut down this tree, it's the last thing that's bearing fruit in the kingdom," said Holly in disbelief. "We're all going to starve if he's allowed to continue." Woogle nodded, her beautiful big eyes full of tears.

The two children didn't like to see the wise old owl crying. They sat with their backs against the trunk of the pear tree and looked sadly at the ground. Pip was never sad for long but he kept looking down because he didn't want to upset the others. Then he noticed something moving on the ground. He bent his head down closer to get a better look. It was a wiggling line; a wiggling line of ants! Each ant was following another and they were all marching in step towards the pear tree. He looked closer and to his surprise saw that the ants were all walking towards a small door at the bottom of the tree. Pip peered down as one after the other the ants tramped under the door. Pip brought his eye down to see even closer. The very last ant in the line turned to look up at Pip. It stuck out its little ant tongue and made a very rude gesture with its antennae and disappeared from view.

"Did you see that?" he said to the others, as he reached out a curious finger.

"Don't touch anything!" cried Woogle when she saw what Pip was pointing at. "That's a Flutter Door."

Pip and Holly looked at Woogle.

"They move about," explained Woogle. "To let insects in and out."

The three of them crowded round it on their hands and knees. (Though for Woogle it was more wings and claws!)

"That's funny," said Holly thoughtfully. "This Flutter Door seemed small until we came closer to look at it, but now it's the same size as us!" She looked back at the garden, which now seemed rather big and towered above them. But the others didn't seem to hear her.

"There's something else about Flutter Doors," murmured Woogle. "They only appear when you need them. PIP! Don't do that!"

But it was too late. Pip had already opened the small door and was squeezing through it.

"Please stop," said the exasperated old owl, "before you get into any trouble. That door leads somewhere that no human is allowed."

"Awesome!" said Pip, only his bottom now visible. "Sounds like the place for me!" And he promptly pushed further through.

"Pip!" cried Holly. "Come back!" But there was no reply. They stared at the little door in anxious silence. "Now we'll have to go after him," said Holly.

"But if we do that we may not be able to come back," said Woogle. "They have rules about this kind of thing."

"Who's they?" said Holly.

Woogle looked worried, "I'm not supposed to say. But . . ."

"But what?" pressed Holly.

"Well . . . I don't know why I didn't think of this before! They might be able to help with our Parip problem."

"Then it's a risk we'll just have to take," said Holly. "King Parip is going to cut this tree down tomorrow morning. We've got to find a way to stop him or the whole kingdom is done for."

And with that she followed Pip through the door.

Chapter 6

A VERY SECRET PLACE

Through the door there was a tunnel hollowed out of the tree trunk. Down and down and round and round the tunnel spiralled while the light in front of Holly gradually got brighter and brighter. And with every step she took, Holly felt as though she was shrinking and growing at the same time. As if she was being stretched and squeezed all over. "I don't think this is a good idea," Woogle's voice echoed mournfully down the stairs.

Finally Holly emerged into bright light and held a hand up to shield her eyes.

Pip was gazing with his mouth wide open. "It's amazing!" he said. And, when Holly and Woogle's eyes had adjusted, their mouths fell open in wonder too.

"Wow!" said Holly.

"Wowee!" said Woogle. Holly and Pip looked at each other and giggled.

A warm golden light lit the world and the air was full of a glorious buzzing. The space in front of them seemed vast, with rolling countryside as far as they could see. The fields were tall with ripe corn and wheat, and all the trees were laden with juicy fruits of all kinds.

"It's just like Stur used to be, but even bigger and better!" said Pip.

"So now we've seen it," said Woogle. "Thank goodness there's no one around. Let's go!"

"No," said Holly. "This might help us stop King Parip. It has to be worth a shot. Right, Pip?"

But Pip didn't hear her. He was looking at the branches of a tree, which were almost breaking under the weight of so much fruit. Holly joined him and they ran from tree to tree, picking apples and pears, oranges and bananas. A buzzing sound made Holly look up and point. "Is that the sun?" she asked. "Why is it making that noise?"

The warm glowing light was just ahead of them.

"Bees!" exclaimed Pip. "That's a sun made up of billions of shining bees."

It was a honey-bee sun, dripping with golden rays and basking the countryside in a honey-yellow glow.

"Come on," said Pip, running towards the light.

"Shsssh!" whispered Woogle. "They'll hear you!"

They tiptoed up the hill, passing a sign that said:

The children looked nervously at each other but, curious to see what was on the other side of the ridge, they pressed on. The closer they got to the top of the hill, the brighter and warmer the honey-bee sun became. They began to hear a rumble of noise, and then the odd cheer or boo.

"What on earth could it be?" asked Pip. Holly shrugged her shoulders. They dropped down and crawled the last few inches until they could peep over the hilltop to see what was happening below.

Chapter 7
THE GREAT GAME

Looking down, they couldn't believe their eyes. Directly below the honey-bee sun was a giant chequered space divided up into dark and light squares. Two ranks of creatures were lined up opposite two more ranks of creatures. At the centre was a large queen bee with her king. On the other side an equally large queen ant with her king.

Pip, who was good at counting, quickly calculated the dark and light chequered squares.

"Sixty-four!" he announced, a little too loudly. He counted again. "And thirty-two squares have creatures on!"

"Shhh," said Woogle, "there's danger here."

"But what are they doing?" asked Holly.

"Let's watch," Pip replied.

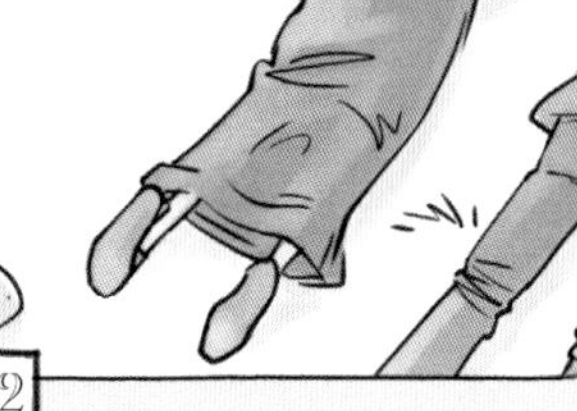

Grandstands, which were packed with every garden creature you can imagine, surrounded three sides of the chequered space. There were bees, butterflies and beetles, ants, worms and moths. There were also snails and grasshoppers and plenty more. On the fourth side was a curious cage with bars all around it and on top of it was a sign saying, THE CLINK.

"What's going on?" Holly whispered to Woogle.

"I told you to be quiet," hissed Woogle. "Humans are not welcome here!"

"So who are they?" said Pip, pointing towards the queens standing beside their kings.

"They are the rulers here," said Woogle. "The queens have ancient traditions. I think this is some kind of strange dance. Keep down. Don't let them see you."

You could not mistake the queen bee standing on her square. She was magnificent, alarming and beautiful. All around her, servants swarmed to bring her anything she wanted.

"The queen of the bees," said Holly, open-mouthed.

She had a long cloak, fine wings and a sun-kissed tan. Her handsome husband sat next to her, on his throne, wearing a golden military uniform.

The queen bee pointed a long finger and one of the creatures on a square moved.

"Look!" said Holly, "there's another queen. The queen of the ants!" And sure enough on the opposite side of the chequered space was the magnificent queen of the ants, next to her king.

Holly and Pip watched, mystified and open-mouthed, as the two queens ordered the creatures to move. Worms and slugs, grasshoppers and crickets, ladybirds and woodlice, sitting on upside-down flowerpots, and ants and bees, all moved to their royal command.

"It doesn't look like a dance to me," whispered Holly. "It looks more like some kind of battle."

"And look, some of them are sent to the Clink," added Pip.

He was right. If a bug was landed on by another, it trudged off to the cage, and was put in the Clink. After each move, the crowded grandstand either booed or cheered, depending on which side they were supporting.

Holly and Pip kept looking at each other and Woogle in disbelief. But they were careful not to make a noise, as they were very worried about what might happen if they were discovered. After quite a lot of bugs had left the board for the Clink, the queen of the ants commanded a woodlouse on a flowerpot to move forward.

Pip and Holly could see lots of little woodlouse legs underneath the flowerpot and it teetered forwards until it crashed into the queen bee and knocked her over.

"Ouch!" she cried.

Holly winced. "That looked painful," she whispered to Pip.

"Shsssh!" hissed Woogle. "They'll hear you."

"You're off," laughed the queen of the ants. "Get to the Clink!"

Half the bugs cheered madly. "And by the way, that's check," said the king ant smugly.

"I wonder what check is?" said Holly. "It's obviously important!"

The king bee scuttled one square forward on his throne.

"Got you!" yelled the queen ant as she moved several squares forward. "Checkmate! Wherever you move, I can take you next go. I win, you loser!"

Half the stands went crazy with delight. "WINNER! WINNER! WINNER!" they chanted.

"IT'S NOT A DANCE, IT'S A BATTLE GAME. THE SQUARES ARE MAKING UP A BOARD!" shouted Holly over the noise, but it had suddenly stopped, and her voice carried over the entire area.

Everybody turned to look up at them. Holly, Pip and Woogle were frozen in fear. What was going to happen now?

Chapter 8

THE GAME EXPLAINED

The Clink doors swung open and the queen of the bees stepped out. She beckoned them with a wave of her arm. They stumbled down the hill.

"Who are you? And what are you doing in our kingdom?" she asked.

"I can explain," said Woogle.

"Let's just throw them in the Clink!" said the queen of the ants impatiently.

"No, we must hear what they have to say," replied the queen of the bees.

"Very well. But this had better be good," said the ant queen reluctantly.

Woogle explained everything: the Flutter Door appearing; about King Marra's care of the land and worry for his son; how things had got all messed up; and what King Parip was planning to do to the pear tree in the morning.

"If he cuts down the pear tree nothing will ever grow in Stur again," said the queen of the bees. "You see, the insects of the garden are commanded by us. They have returned here because there is no food in Stur. If the tree is cut down, the Flutter Door will go, and the way will be lost forever. Our creatures will not go back to your world and pollinate your plants or help enrich the soil and everything will die. But that is no matter to us! We don't need you, we have everything we need. It's your own fault for having such a stupid king. Now you have seen our secret game, we cannot let you leave."

"But we can't stay here," begged Holly. "What about our parents?"

"Our rules are clear," said the queen bee. "Any trespassers must stay here forever in the Clink! You've ruined Stur, we don't want you bringing your nasty king here and ruining our special kingdom, too."

"The Clink! The Clink! The Clink!" the crowd chanted at the tops of their voices, in a strange kind of frenzy.

Holly turned to Pip and Woogle. "What shall we do?"

Woogle looked worried, but Pip suddenly smiled. "I've got it," he said. And then he leaned forward and whispered in Holly's ear. She shook her head doubtfully, but then she shrugged her shoulders and turned back to the two waiting queens.

"We challenge you!" said Holly, so loudly that everyone could hear, "to a GAME!"

"Challenge accepted!" cried the queen bee. "If you lose, you will never see your home again. If you win, we will let you return to your world. And if you can win without capturing any of my pieces, I will give you one wish as well."

Holly, Pip and Woogle looked at each other in slight panic. "We'll never do it," said Woogle.

Holly shook her head. "If we don't win we'll have to stay here and if the tree is cut down we we won't be able to stop King Parip, and everyone in Stur will starve." She clenched her fists with determination. "We have to win!" But then she sighed. "The trouble is, we don't even know how to play the game."

Pip pointed to the notice on the large scoreboard. "These might be a help," he said.

"It's the best place to start," said a squeaky voice from behind them. They turned to see the cheeky ant Pip had followed into the kingdom. "I'll show you around if you like."

Holly and Pip nodded eagerly but Woogle was more cautious. "Be careful, children," she whispered.

The Rules

How to play Chess

Aim of the Game:

To checkmate the
other side's king!

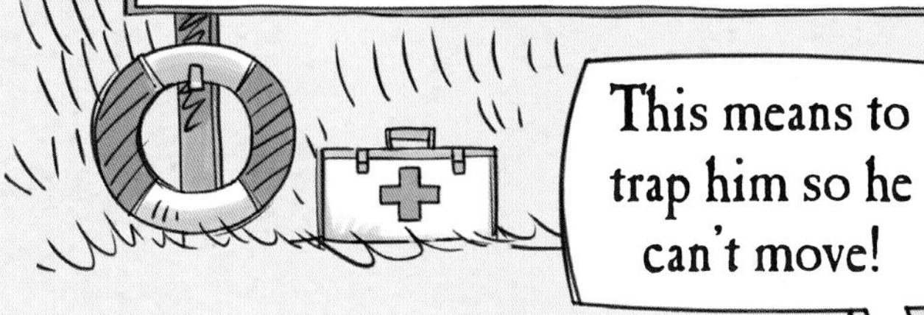

You can also learn and play chess with the Foolish King app!
Or you can play at www.thefoolishking.com

The board:

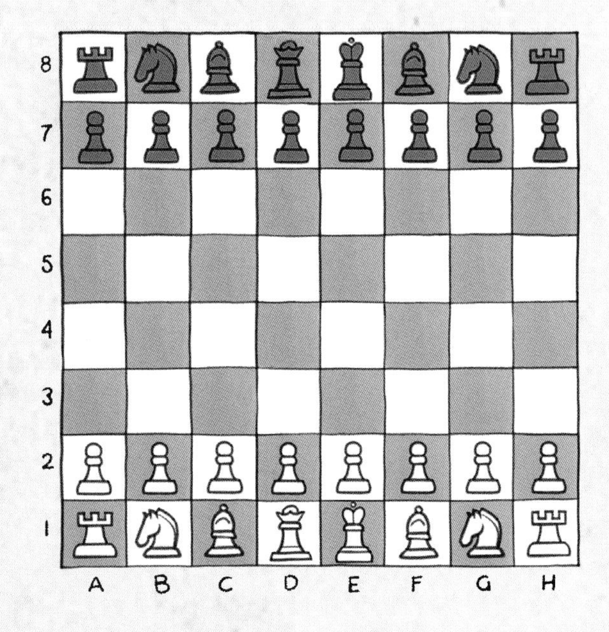

1. Numbers run down the side, letters across the bottom.
2. Set up the board so that the square closest to each player's right hand is light coloured.
3. The pieces start in these positions:

How to play:

1. The light colour always starts!
2. Each player takes it in turn to move a piece.
3. You always have to move a piece on your turn. You can't skip your go!
4. You can't move your piece through a square with another of your pieces on it!
5. If you move your piece onto a square occupied by your opponent's piece, you 'take' them, and remove them from the board. You can only take one piece per turn.
6. You can't 'take' your opponent's king. We'll explain him later!
7. Ants and Bees (footsoldiers) have a special way of 'taking' an opponent's pieces – we'll explain that later too!

How to win:

1. The winner is the player who traps their opponent's king, so that he can't move without being taken! This is called being 'checkmated'.
2. If neither king can be put in checkmate by the pieces left on the board, the game is a draw.

"Come on, then," said the ant. "Here's a run through of the moves before we get started."

How the pieces move:

Ant and Bees! ♟

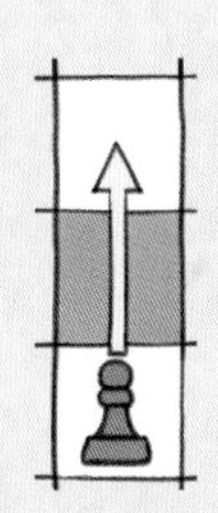

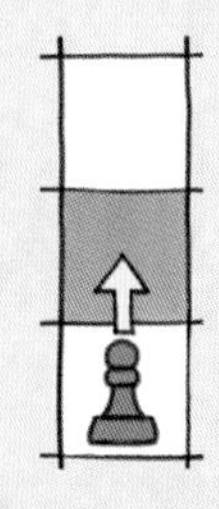

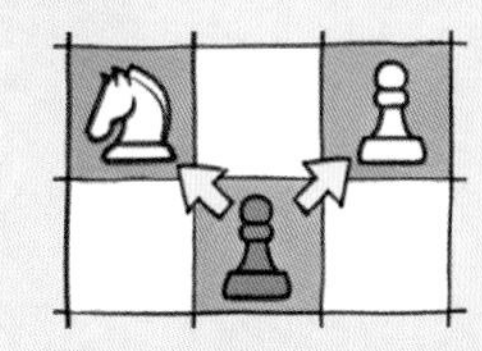

1. Ants and bees are the footsoldiers.
2. On their first move they can move one or two squares forward, straight ahead only.
3. After their first move, they can only move one square forward.
4. If there is a piece in front of them, they have to stop.
5. They can't take a piece by moving forward!
6. They never move sideways or backwards.
7. They can only take pieces by moving diagonally forward – see the picture!
8. They also have a special ability – if they can reach the last row at the opposite side of the board, they can be transformed into any piece you like, except for the king (so you can have an extra queen or extra knight – but not an extra king!).

Grasshoppers and Crickets! 

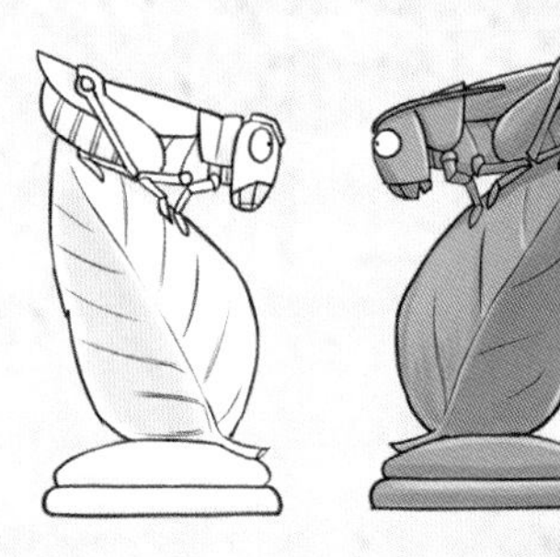

They always move 3 steps, in an 'L' shape. The 'L' can point in any direction. They are the only piece that can jump over other pieces.

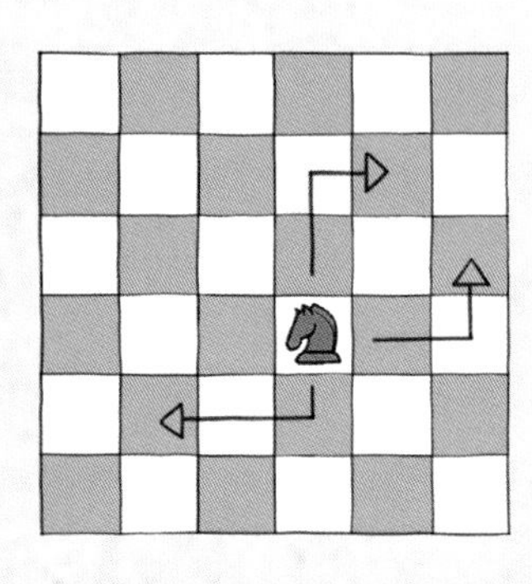

Worms and Slugs! 

These can move diagonally backward or forward as many squares as they want.

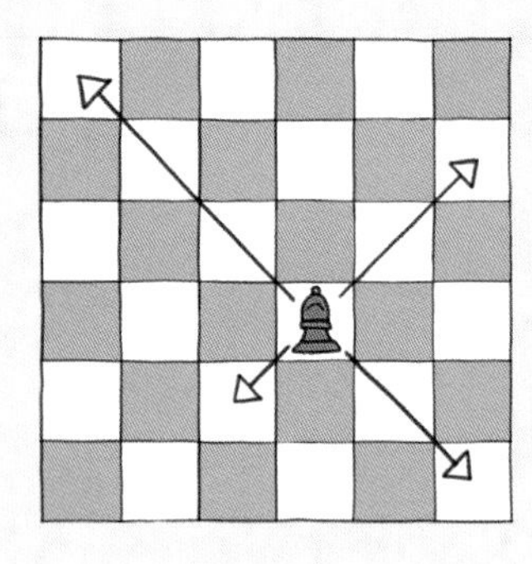

Ladybirds and Woodlice! 

These move in a straight line, forward, backward, or sideways, for as many squares as they want, but they can't move diagonally.

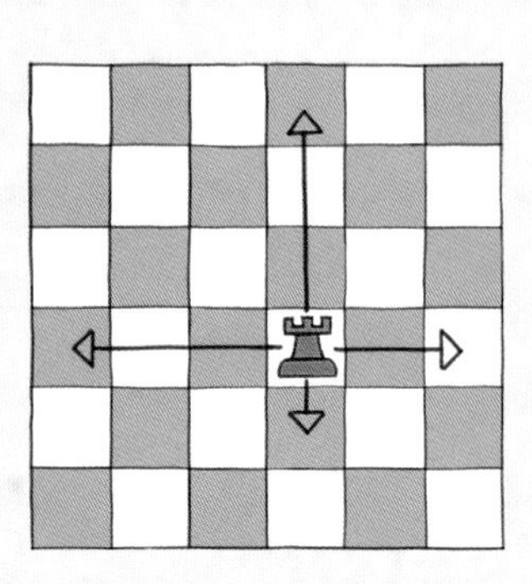

The Queen 

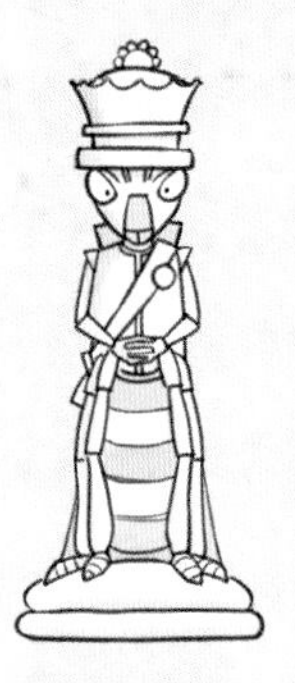

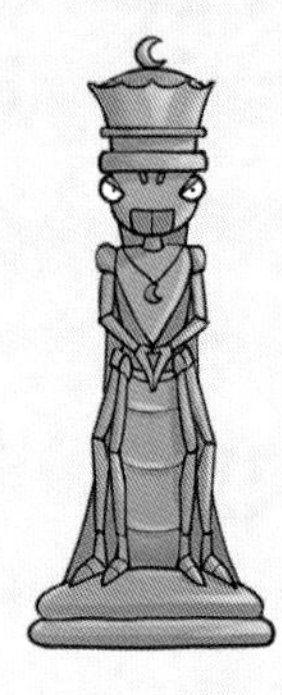

She can move in any direction in a straight line for as many squares as she wants, including diagonally!

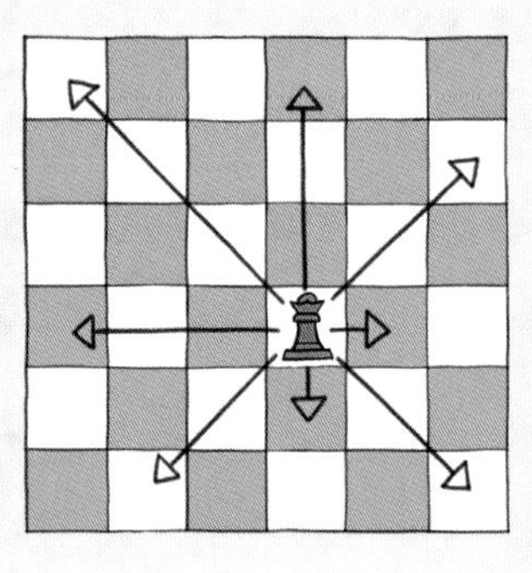

The King ♚

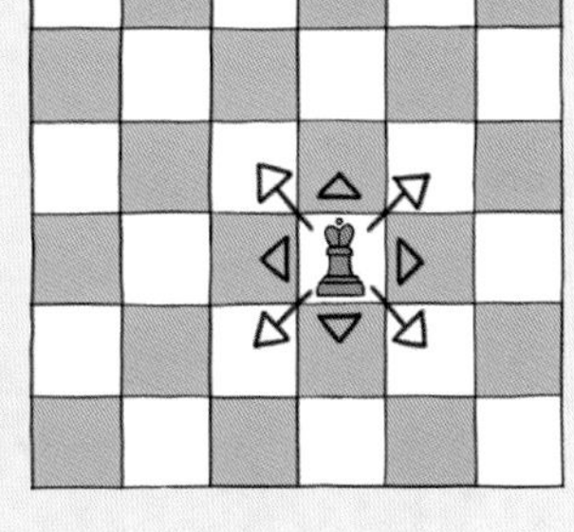

- He can move in any direction, but can only move one square at a time.
- He cannot be taken.
- If a piece moves so that they could take the king on their next turn, the king is in 'check'.
- The king must be protected! Either the king must move, or you must find a way to remove or block the piece that has checked the king.
- If you can't move the king to safety, he is in 'checkmate', and you have lost the game!

Castling:

This is a special move that the king and a ladybird/ woodlouse can make, but only if NEITHER of them has moved yet AND there aren't any other pieces in between them!

When castling, the king also can't start on, end on or move through any space that is threatened by an enemy piece!

To castle, the king moves two spaces towards the ladybird/ woodlouse, and the ladybird/ woodlouse jumps to the other side of the king!

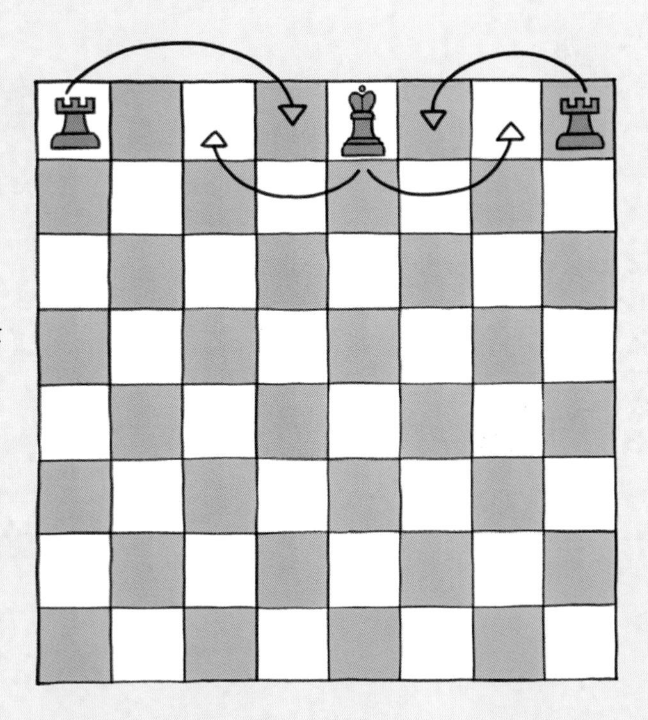

Chapter 9

ANTS AND BEES (footsoldiers)

Holly and Pip moved around to see the first training board. A sign by the side of it read "Ants and Bees Training Camp."

Just like the main board, the training board was divided into dark and light squares.

The ants stood in a line on the second row, filling all of the squares. Green leaves were scattered around the board, together with what looked like tiny anteaters.

"Right, you horrible little ants," shouted a larger-than-usual ant with a cane under one leg.

"This is our battle plan," he said, pointing to a picture on a large chart showing squares and arrows.

"First move can be one or two squares forward. Then after that, one square forward. You must never move backwards – footsoldiers never retreat!" he shouted. "So," he added. "How do we capture our enemy?"

"If they are on the square diagonally in front of you, sergeant major," said a large ant at the front.

"Well done, son, and what do you become if you reach the end of the board?" asked the sergeant major.

"Er . . . er . . . oh, I know . . . a butterfly!" shouted a younger ant.

"NO!" said the sergeant major, shaking his head and looking very disappointed. "What did we say before?"

"Oh, sorry, I meant any player you want to be except the king," said the ant. But then he looked to the ant next to him and muttered. "I always wanted to be a butterfly though."

"Well done, my boy, yes, you can start to move like any one of those back-row glory boys. Now that's worth training for!"

"And defeating the daytime bugs," added the ant.

"That's my boy," said the sergeant major, with a twinkle in his eye.

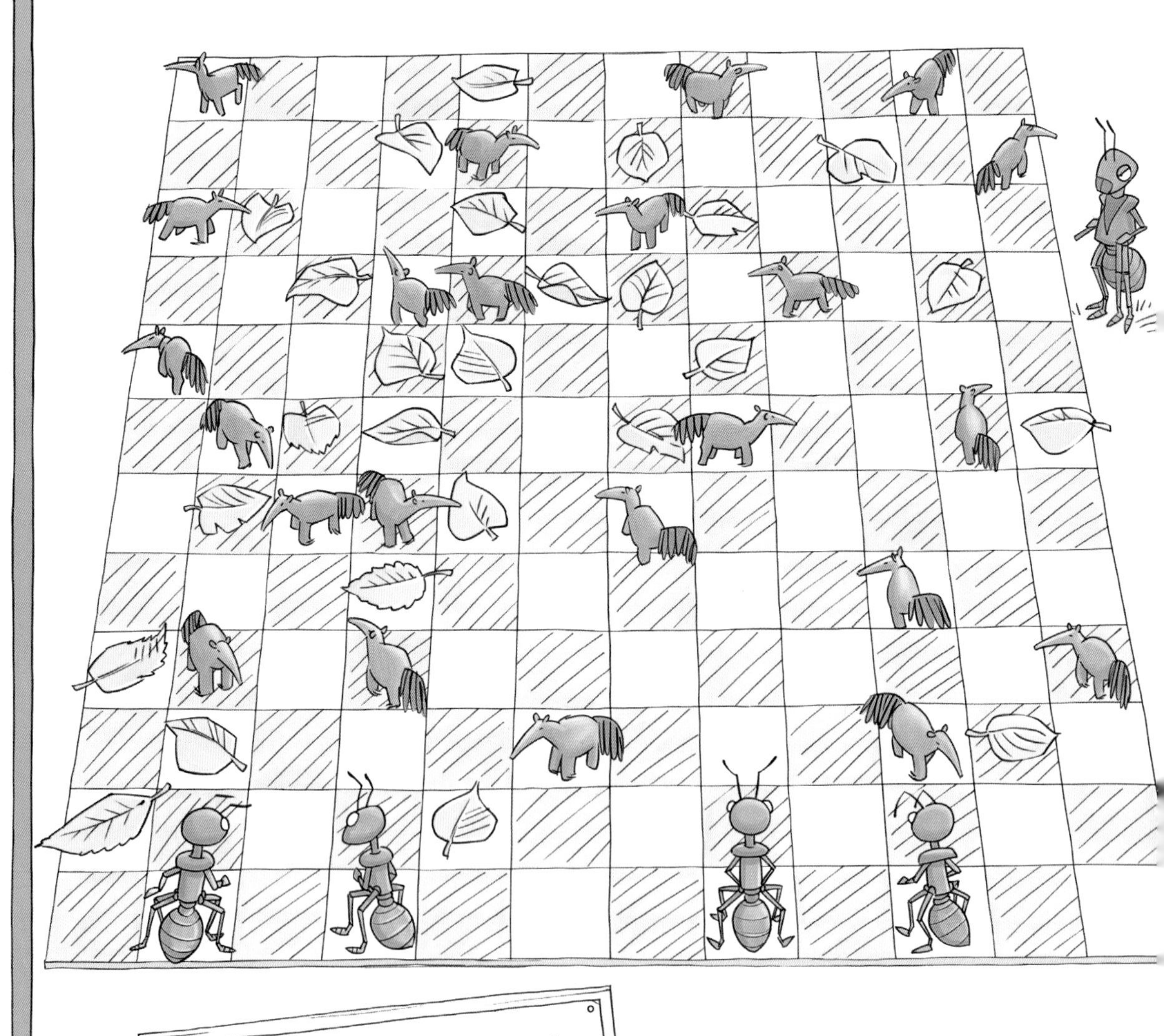

Remember, footsoldiers can only move forward one square per turn. You can only move one square diagonally if it helps you get to a leaf to eat. Start again if you touch an anteater.

"Now, my lovely lads, today we will practise just on the white starting squares. You ants on the dark squares move to the side.

"With that, the ants on the dark squares marched off the board. "Now, listen to me. You remaining ants must get to the far side of the board. I want you to pick up those juicy green leaves as you cross, but only if they are on a square diagonally in front of you. If you land on a square with an anteater on, it's curtains!"

Holly and Pip stood and watched while the ants started to cross the board. "I think I've got it," whispered Holly.

A little ant about to make his first move winked at her and gave a small nod. As he did, their helpful guide reached up on tiptoes and whispered something into Holly's ear. She listened carefully and then gasped. "Ok! Thank you!"

Holly's tip (as told by her guide): start with a footsoldier standing in front of the king or queen to allow your back row pieces to move out and begin to control the centre of the board.

Chapter 10

WORMS AND SLUGS

Holly, Pip, Woogle and the friendly ant went to the next practice board. The sign by the board read "Diagonally is Best!"

Two worms squirmed on the back row, three squares in from each side. One was on a dark square and one on a white square. They looked very nervous. Scattered around the board were bars in the ground in the place of white and dark squares. Every now and again a bird's beak popped through the bars, followed by a squawk.

"Now, worms," said a large green grass snake. "You must move diagonally, forward or backwards to get to the lovely dung on the other side of the board. Now, make sure you don't go over the crow pits – those birds are hungry today!"

The worms gulped and very carefully started to move diagonally forward and back, avoiding the bird traps, to reach the other side.

"I hope they don't get eaten," whispered Holly to Pip.

"They can only move diagonally," said Pip. "I don't fancy their chances."

"But don't you see?" said Woogle, getting excited. "The moves are also teaching them how to be good gardeners. Each insect has its own special moves and working together helps them garden."

"You're right," said their guide, "we can only move in certain ways!"

"That must be why everything grows so well here," said Holly.

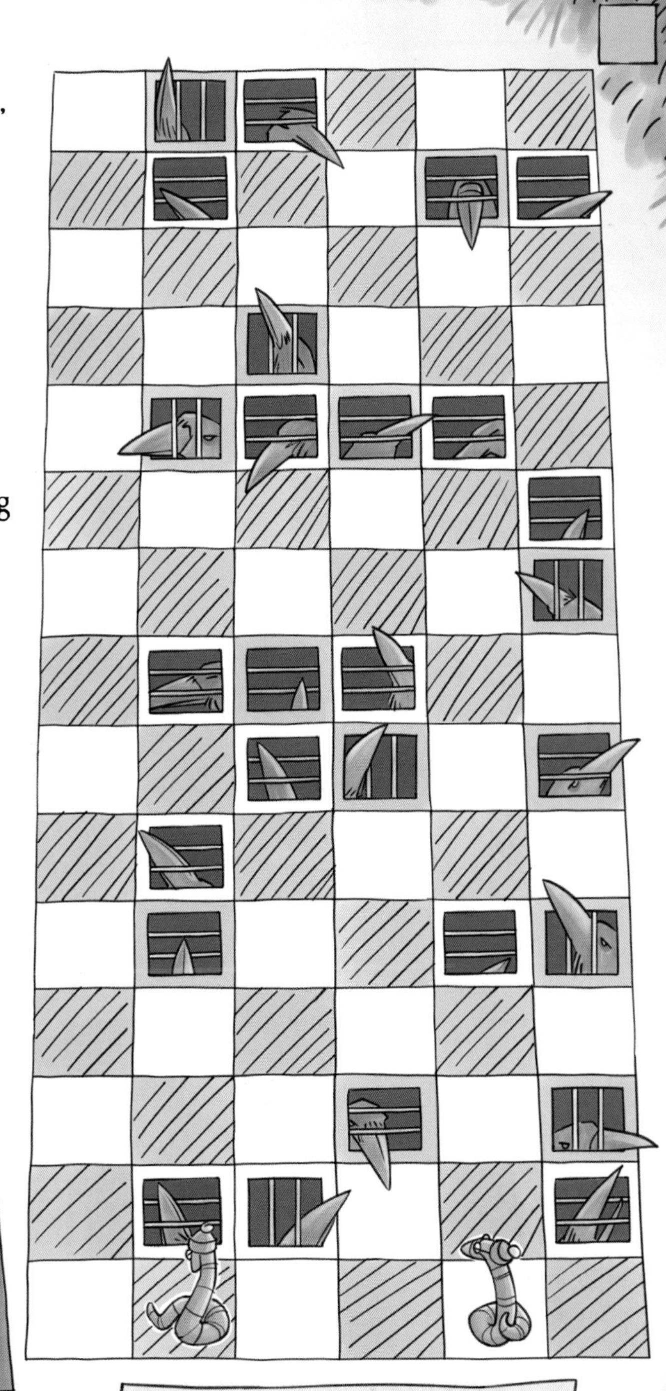

Remember, these pieces move diagonally backward and forward for as many squares as they like. Help the worms find a way across the board. When you reach a dead end, you can change direction, but be sure to avoid the bird traps!

Holly's tip (as told by her guide): worms and slugs are best held back until after your grasshoppers and crickets have moved.

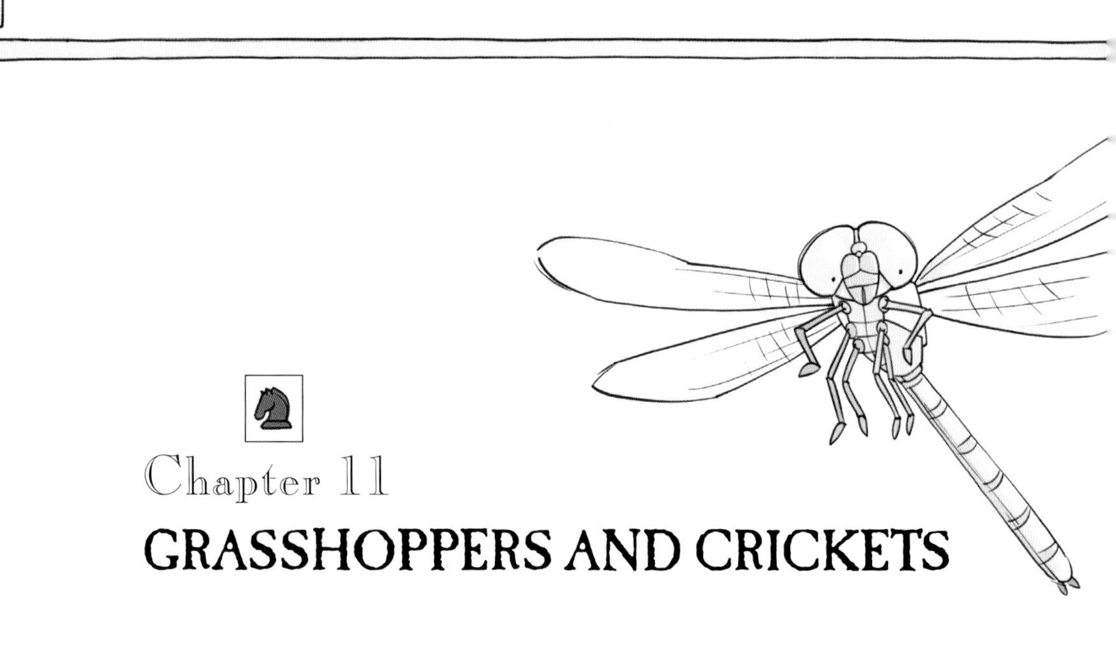

Chapter 11

GRASSHOPPERS AND CRICKETS

The four moved to the next board, which had been filled with water. Lily pads were dotted from one side to the other. The sign by the board said "Grasshoppers and Crickets."

The grasshoppers lined up in front of a dragonfly, who was teaching them. "Now, follow my routine. Two steps forward, one to the side. Then one to the side and two steps back."

To begin with, the grasshoppers didn't do very well at all, and crashed into each other, but after a while they got the moves perfectly. Rising into the air they moved forward two steps, then hovered, and one to the side. Or one forward, and two to the side. And backwards as well.

"Very well, you are now ready for the pond test. First two please – and remember all I have told you," said the dragonfly.

"I'll go first," said a cocky grasshopper. "I'll show you how easy it is and that we don't need your silly training." With that he hopped onto the lily pad on the back row, one square from the edge.

"Now you need to get to the other side of the board by just landing on the lily pads. Please don't land in the water," implored the dragonfly.

The grasshopper nonchalantly lifted off the pad and moved two squares forward and one to the side, landing effortlessly on another lily pad.

"Easy peasy," he said, already taking off for his next move. But he misjudged his move of one forward and two to the side and landed just short of the lily pad. A huge tongue rose out of the water and pulled him under!

"Where has he gone?" asked another grasshopper in a panic.

"He'll have been eaten by a large frog," said the dragonfly, with a tear in his eye. "I hate losing my pupils like that."

The next grasshopper to go was a lot less confident, and concentrated fully as he leapt high for every move, until he hit the lily pad on the far side of the pond.

Holly and Pip sighed in relief. "Thank goodness for that," said Holly, "I didn't want to see another go under."

"Splendid, splendid," clapped the dragonfly. "I think you will be perfect for tonight's game."

Holly's tip (as told by her guide): put grasshoppers and crickets near the centre of the board as early as you can. From there they will have the greatest number of squares to attack. Grasshoppers and crickets and worms are as useful as about three bees or ants (footsoldiers).

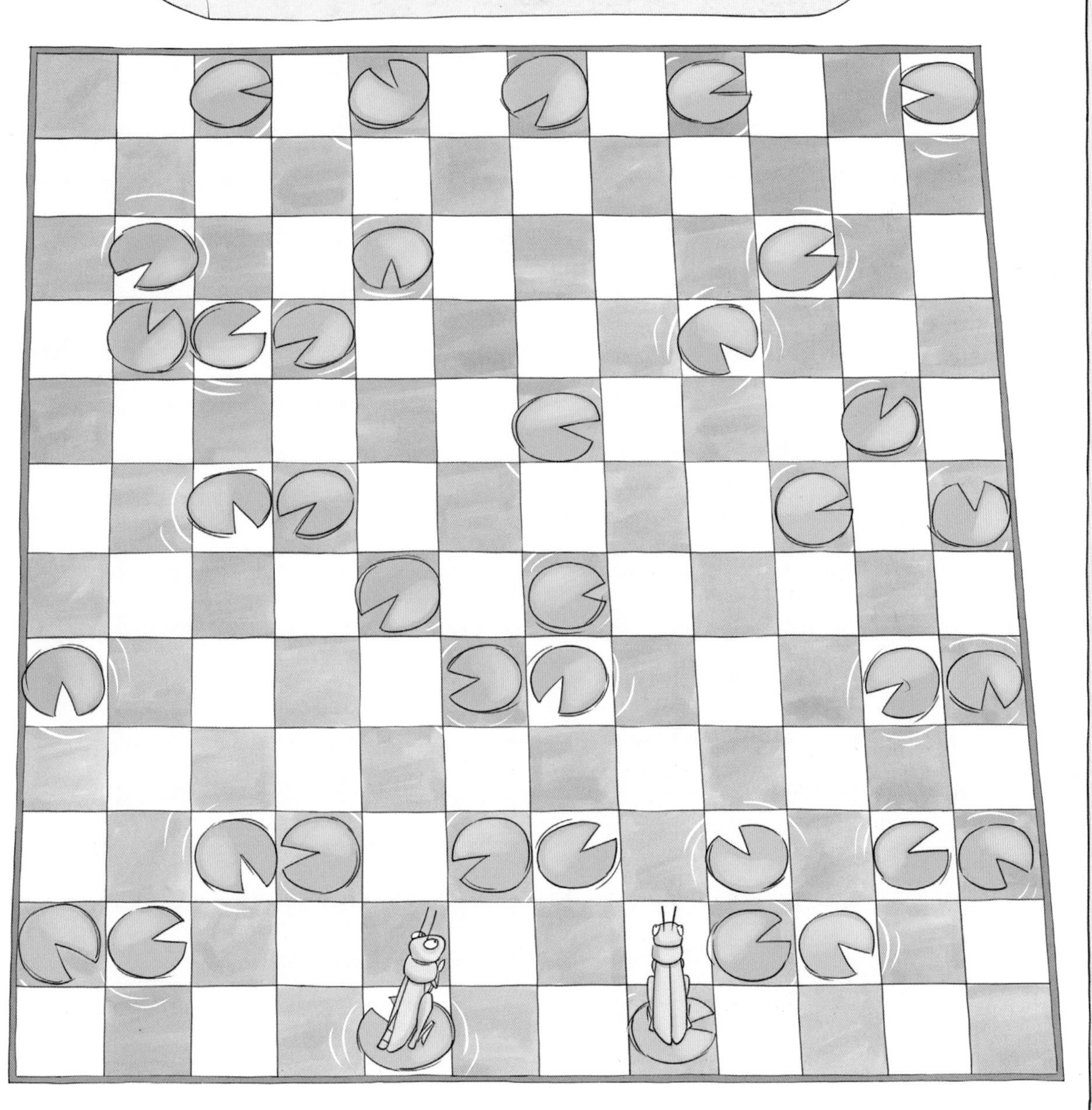

"Come on," said Holly. "The day is going too quickly. Let's move to the next board."

Chapter 12
LADYBIRDS AND WOODLICE

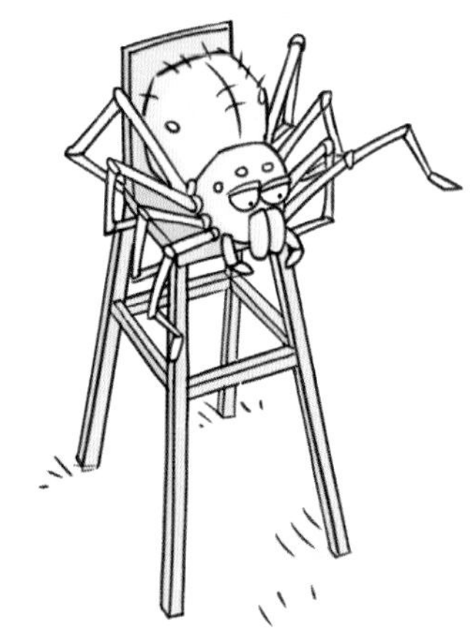

This time the board had little brick walls built on some of the squares. The sign at the side said "Ladybirds and Woodlice".

Underneath, a picture showed that ladybirds and woodlice could move in straight lines, forward and back, and side to side for as many squares as they liked.

Holly and Pip watched as a ladybird sat on top of a small upturned terracotta pot. "Forward," the ladybird shouted. With that, the pot raised fractionally off the ground, to reveal dozens of little ladybird legs. The flowerpot teetered forward, wobbling from side to side as the ladybird hung on. The flowerpot began to gather pace.

"Slow down, slow down!" shouted the ladybird. But it was too late – the pot crashed into a brick wall three squares in front.

"No, no, no!" screamed a large hairy spider sitting in a high chair next to the scoreboard. "You need to get to the other side of the board without hitting any walls. Now get up, find a new pot and try again!"

The ladybirds struggled to their feet and collected a new flowerpot.

"It is very important for you to stay on the board, as ladybirds and woodlice are powerful and can command the battlefield," explained the spider.

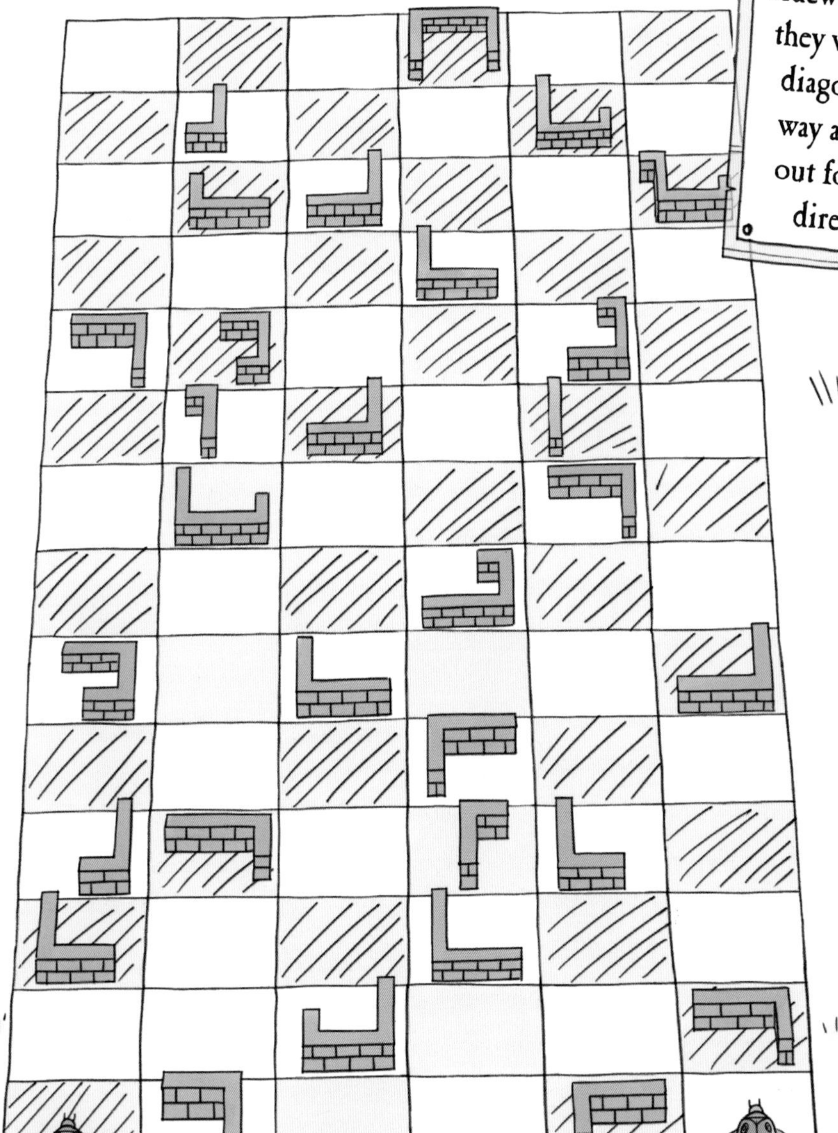

Remember, ladybirds and woodlice move in a straight line, forward, backwards or sideways for as many squares as they want, but they can't move diagonally. Help them find a way across the board – look out for the walls and change direction to avoid them!

Holly's tip (as told by her guide): ladybirds and woodlice are the most important pieces next to the queen. They are as useful as five ants and bees (footsoldiers). Use your ladybirds and woodlice to protect the king by castling. Look back to p.45 to see how castling works.

Chapter 13

THEIR ROYAL MAJESTIES

Holly, Pip, Woogle and the ant had seen enough and inched towards the last board, which was much more splendid than the others. A throne sat at one end and a red carpet surrounded the board. The noticeboard read:

The queen bee and her king walked hand in hand towards the edge of the board. On the squares in front of them were diamonds, swords and pools of mud. A smartly dressed official explained that the king should move one square at a time, collecting swords, until he reached the other side, and his queen must do the same landing on squares with diamonds on.

"However, Your Majesties, you **MUST** avoid the squares of mud, which will get your royal clothes very messy."

Holly and Pip watched them move around the board in all directions until eventually they reached the other side.

"Can you tell us why they said 'check' and 'checkmate' in the game?" Holly asked their guide.

The ant nodded and explained, "Check is what you must say if your opponent's king is in danger of being taken. Checkmate is what you say if the king is unable to move out of danger and therefore you can take him and end the game."

Holly's tip (as told by her guide): don't get the king and queen into play too early as you might accidentally put them in danger. Get other pieces into the game first to ensure the king and queen's safety. The king's safety is critical.

Remember, the queen can move in any direction in a straight line for as many squares as she pleases, including diagonally. The king can move in any direction, but only one square at a time! Help them find a way across the board. The queen can pick up diamonds and the king can collect the swords. Make sure they don't fall into the pools of mud!

The queen bee and her king finished their training and walked over to the children.

"So, how are you getting on?" asked the queen imperiously.

"Quite well, actually," said Holly, because she was beginning to understand how to play the game. "There's only one thing I'm unsure about."

"What's that?" the queen asked.

"Why do you play this game in the first place?" asked Holly.

"Yes, what's the point?" added Pip.

The queen paused for a moment and then began to speak.

"Long ago, the insects of the day and the night would fight each other every morning when the sun came up, and every evening when the moon rose. For that short time each day, both day and night bugs would be awake, and looking for food. But in their fighting over food many were killed and so there were fewer insects to tend the plants. I ruled the creatures of the day and the queen ant commanded the insects at night and we agreed to play this game instead. Not only did the game stop the insects killing each other, it also helped their gardening skills. The gardens grew, and more and more insects were born. So many that some went to visit your world and help make more food grow there."

"Who made the game up?" asked Holly.

"We did," replied the queen. "We looked at the way our different creatures moved, and worked together to make up the rules."

"I see," said Holly thoughtfully. "Please can we have some time to prepare now?" she asked the queen bee.

The queen bee shook her head. "NO. I'm afraid not. There's no time. The moon is about to rise, the day and night creatures must play now!"

As she spoke, the honey-bee sun dissolved, as millions of bees flew to their homes to rest. Their place was taken by millions of fireflies, whose silvery beams spread over the fields, waking the nighttime insects from their slumbers.

Chapter 14
THE GAME

Holly and Pip have taken over from the queen and king of the nighttime bugs!

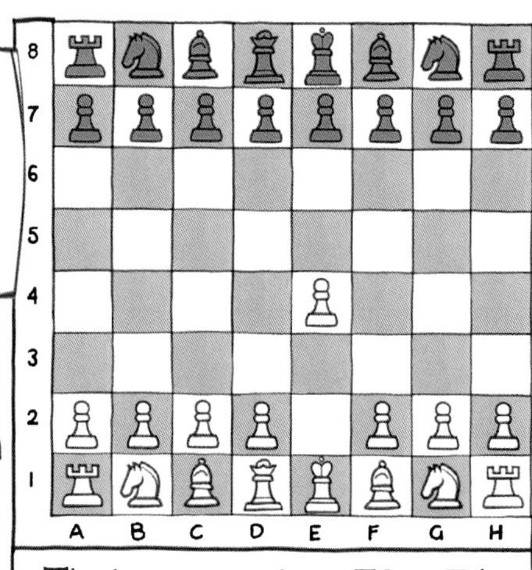

The bee moves from E2 to E4

Ant moves E7 to E5

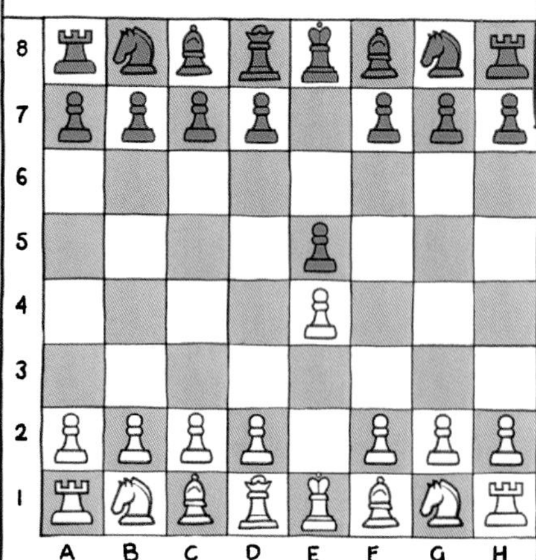

Bee moves F2 to F3

We've got an opening, look!
Mr Slug, could you move out?
Slug moves F8 to C5
Come on! We need to make room! Step forward!
Bee moves B2 to B3
Mr Cricket, jump out too, please!
Cricket moves G8 to F6
Blast off! Here I go!

Worm moves C1 to B2
They're bringing out their big players. I don't like that.
This'll show them how to really play!
Look! If we move the worm there, we can take that ant next go!
Quick, Mr Cricket! You need to protect our ant!
Cricket moves B8 to C6
Don't worry, I'm here!
Worm moves F1 to C4
We need to match them! Worm, get over there.
Yes, Your Majesty.

Look! We can castle! I saw the king do it this morning, and it'll keep me safe.
Thanks, Woodlouse!
King Pip moves E8 to G8, Woodlouse moves to F8
Grasshopper moves B1 to C3
How did you learn how to do that? Grasshopper, we need you to get involved!
Mr Cricket, move into that space, please!
Here we go again!
Cricket moves F6 to H5

Bee moves G2 to G4
We can't have that. Let's get him. Bee – move!
Let's get you out of the way, Mr Cricket! You'll be safe there!
Cricket moves H5 to F4
Grasshopper moves C3 to A4
They've started to surround us. This looks bad.
Ah ha! I bet they don't notice we can get them with the grasshopper on the next go!

Time for me to get involved!
Check!
Queen Holly moves D8 to H4
We can't have this! You'd better move, darling.
The king moves E1 to F1
I've got you now. Checkmate!
You're right in front of me. I can take you.
Queen Holly moves H4 to F2
I don't think so. Mr Slug is looking after me! It seems you've lost!
Oh. Oh, dear.

The queen and king bee were amazed to have lost to Holly and Pip, and the queen ant, watching on from the stands, looked terribly cross.

"I haven't taken any of your army," said Holly. "Please can I have my wish now?"

"Very well," said the queen bee, still wondering how the children had beaten her.

"I would like to show King Parip how to play your game," wished Holly.

"Absolutely not! This is our secret game, the way in which we train the insects and creatures to grow such amazing gardens," said the queen ant. "It's definitely *not* for humans!"

"I understand," said Holly. "But my dad told me that King Parip loves playing games." She looked over at Woogle, who nodded encouragingly. "I think this might be a way to show King Parip how important it is to look after his kingdom again. And maybe he will reconsider cutting down the pear tree and look after the land again."

"Fat chance," said the queen bee.

"Let her try," said Woogle. "You have nothing to lose."

"We understand that he's not particularly kind to insects," said the queen ant. Woogle bowed her head, feeling embarrassed. "Maybe this will persuade him otherwise," she said, looking at the sceptical queen bee. The queen ant whispered to her, "The Flutter Door appeared to them for a reason, could this be it?"

The queens talked for a while. Then they nodded to the servants, who dragged forward a number of statues resembling the creatures and the kings and queens. "We use these special pieces to play the game when the creatures hibernate in the winter. You can borrow these statues to play with King Parip, but you *must* return them before the snow falls," said the queen bee. "Our creatures will help you carry them to the tree, and you can take them from there."

Holly nodded her agreement. She, Pip and Woogle headed back to the walled garden, followed by the creatures carrying the pieces.

"You'll need this, too," winked their friendly ant, handing Holly a chequered game board.

When they came out of the door, the sun had started to rise. Holly broke into a sprint. "Hurry," she shouted. "We don't have much time!"

Chapter 15

IN THE NICK OF TIME

That morning, as he had promised, King Parip arrived at the Perry's cottage, carrying an axe. Crow banged on the door until a reluctant Mrs Perry opened it. A tired and weary Mr Perry stood up from the kitchen table.

"Well, lead me to the pear tree or tell me how my gardens are going to grow lots of food again!" the king demanded.

"I don't know," said Mr Perry, as he fell to his knees. "Please don't chop the tree down. It's the only tree in the whole kingdom that is bearing fruit."

But then Holly, Pip and Woogle burst through the kitchen door.

"Stop!" said Holly. She was panting for breath, having run all the way.

"Why?" asked King Parip.

"I have an idea," said Holly.

"Don't trust her, sire, it's just a trick. Punish her for interrupting you," suggested Crow.

"Listen to her, Your Majesty," said Woogle, nodding reassuringly.

"If you play a game with me, Your Majesty, I can explain everything," said Holly.

"I'm much too important to play games with you," scoffed the king. But as Holly laid the game out on the table, he began to move over and then, looking closer he sat down.

Holly set the little statues in their starting positions and explained how the different players moved and the game was won. Parip was mesmerised and insisted she showed him how to play at once. As they played, Holly told them how the bugs would practise day and night, directed by the queen bee and the queen ant. And how their practise helped make the garden grow and kept peace within their land.

Not surprisingly, Holly won the game, but VERY surprisingly the king wasn't cross at all.

"This is the best game I have ever played. Let's play again!" he said, because although he hated losing, he wanted a chance to beat Holly at this wonderful new game.

Cutting down the pear tree was forgotten as the king and Holly played again and again. And gradually, the others learnt to play too. It took many weeks, but a change started to come over Parip. He became more patient and thoughtful and started to discuss the gardens with Mr Perry.

Using the game, they talked about the best way to bring Stur back to life, and as Parip's chess game flourished so did Stur. He *never* mentioned cutting the pear tree down again.

All too soon, the seasons changed and the pieces were due to be returned to the insects. Holly and Pip were worried about telling Parip he could no longer play his favourite game but eventually they plucked up the courage.

"The gardens can't grow alone, they need the insects," explained Holly. "And the insects need the statues for the winter."

"I see," said the king, starting to understand that he needed everyone's help. "Will the creatures return to Stur after the winter and play their magical game?" he asked.

"Only if you promise to care for the land with them and share what is grown with everyone. Then everything will grow once again," said Holly.

The king nodded, "We must make copies of these pieces and teach all the people of Stur how to play so in the future this doesn't happen again and we remember how important the insects are."

Parip asked Mr Perry to make boards and playing pieces and for Holly and Pip to tour the country teaching the people to play the magical game which makes things grow. King Parip got the first set of pieces Mr Perry made and played all day and night. The king decided he would award The Golden Pear to the best player.

And so the gardens and fields of Stur started to blossom again, as the farmers and insects returned to work. King Parip so loved playing chess that he began visiting all parts of his kingdom to play it.

The following year Stur had its biggest harvest ever. The barns and cellars were bursting with the finest quality food and, once again, Stur became the richest of all lands.

King Parip rewarded Holly and Pip by making them prince and princess, and the people loved them and the king for his wise choice. The king never married, so when he died, Holly and Pip jointly ruled the Kingdom of Stur. They were great rulers; always interested in the people, the bugs and the land. And the garden game became so famous that people came from all over the world to visit the royal garden to watch a game.

The magical game is still played in gardens everywhere today. If you look extra carefully in the early morning, in a quiet corner of your own garden, you will see the remains of the board from the night before. And if you watch out you will see the bugs practising for their next game amongst the flowers and vegetables.

So that is how the game of chess was invented and then taken to ancient China and India. The board and pieces have changed over time and are the ones you may know today. Kings and queens, bishops and knights have all played this ancient game, but very few of them knew its secret history.

THE END

You can also learn and play chess with the Foolish King app! Or you can play at www.thefoolishking.com

Practice Board solutions

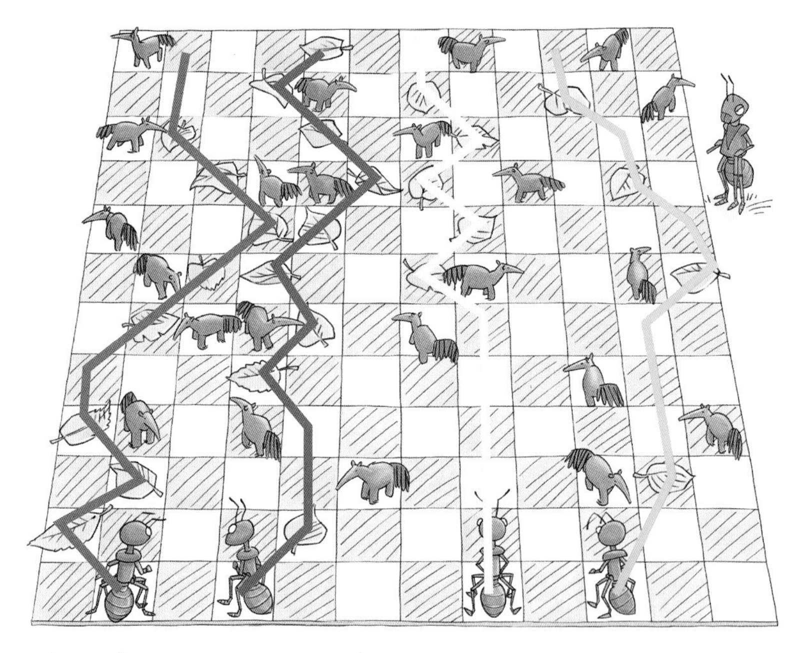

Ants' practice board
Page 48

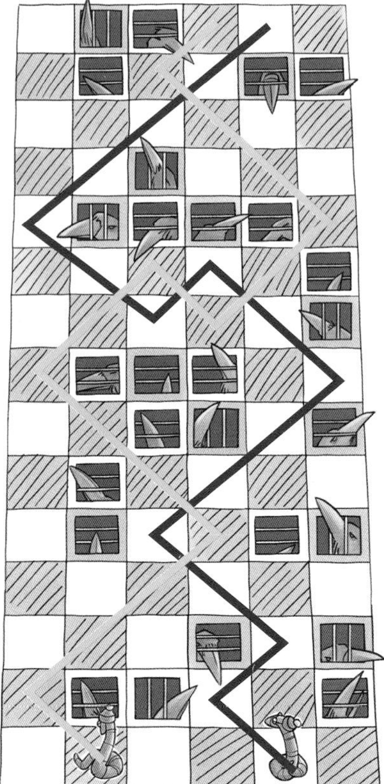

Worms' practice Board
Page 51

Grasshoppers' practice board

Page 55

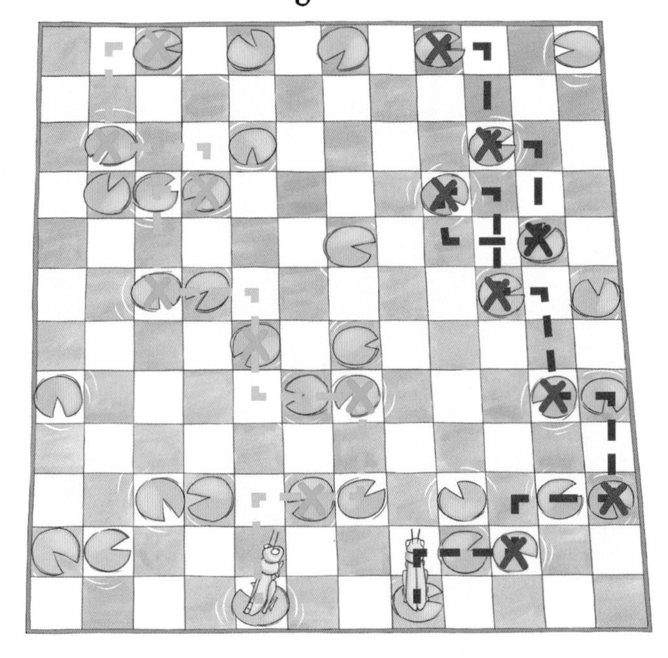

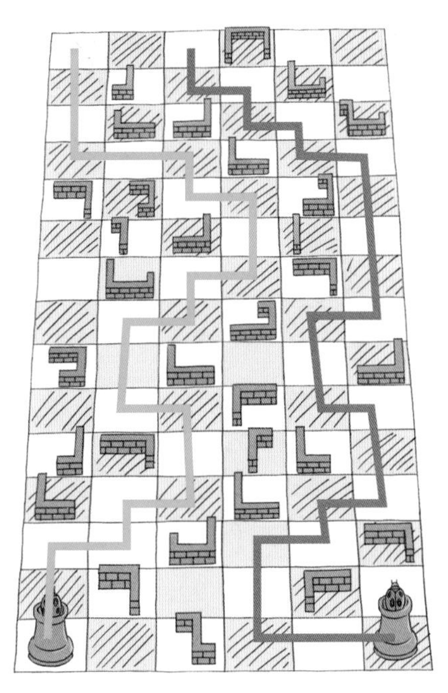

Ladybirds' practice board

Page 57

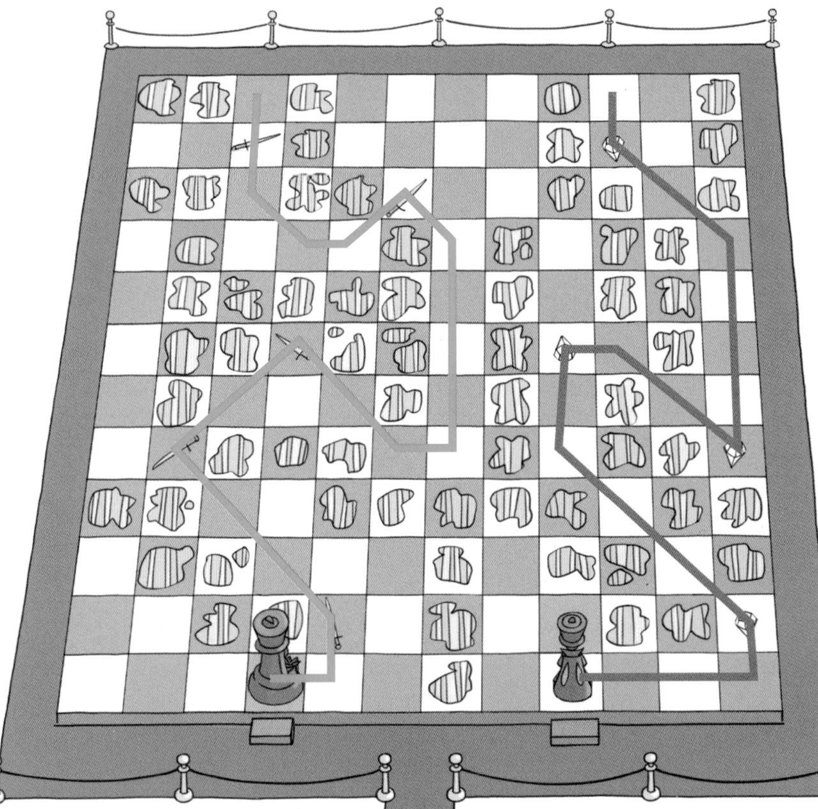

King and queen's practice board

Page 61

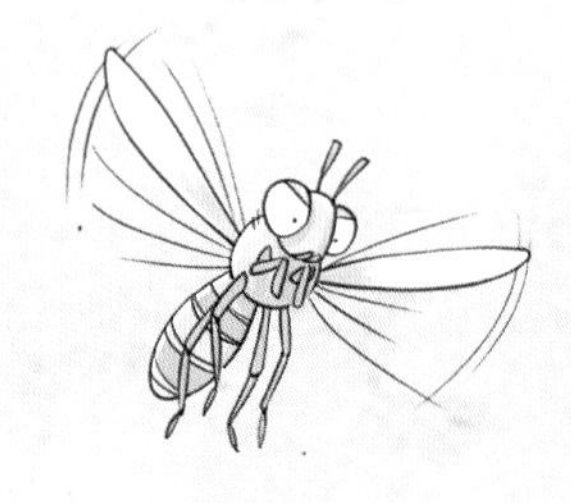

The Foolish King
is a
DAVID FICKLING BOOK

First published in Great Britain in 2016 by
David Fickling Books,
31 Beaumont Street, Oxford, OX1 2NP
www.davidficklingbooks.com

This paperback edition published 2017

Illustrations inked and coloured by Geraint Ford

978-1-910989-86-9
1 3 5 7 9 10 8 6 4 2

WARNING: This book will turn you chess-crazy!

Papers used by David Fickling Books are from well-managed forests and other responsible sources.

DAVID FICKLING BOOKS Reg. No. 8340307

A CIP catalogue record for this book is available from the British Library

Printed and bound by Toppan Leefung